Contents

CW00672173

*B = bronze; S = silver; G = gold; ( ) = the line must be played but cannot be assessed for a Medal.

Levels in bold type indicate that the piece is for mixed saxophones. In each of these cases, the instrumentation is given at the start of the piece. Every other piece can be played either on E flat saxophones or on B flat saxophones.

Dreamy Days

Alan Bullard

© 2005 by The Associated Board of the Royal Schools of Music

Shepherd's Hey

Trad. English arr. Alan Haughton

© 2005 by The Associated Board of the Royal Schools of Music

AB 3140

Sixth Sense

Robert Tucker

© 2005 by The Associated Board of the Royal Schools of Music

Rock-four Cheese

Jeffery Wilson

© 2005 by The Associated Board of the Royal Schools of Music

AB 3140

Control-Alt-Delete

Karen Street

© 2005 by The Associated Board of the Royal Schools of Music

Unsquare Rag

Alan Haughton

© 2005 by The Associated Board of the Royal Schools of Music

AB 3140

Land of Hope and Glory

from *Pomp and Circumstance*, Op. 39 No. 1

Elgar arr. Russell Stokes

© 2005 by The Associated Board of the Royal Schools of Music

AB 3140

Pagan Lament

Colin Cowles

© 2005 by The Associated Board of the Royal Schools of Music

AB 3140

Last Waltz in Bluesville

Gordon Lewin

© 2005 by The Associated Board of the Royal Schools of Music

The Dance Lesson

Karen Street

© 2005 by The Associated Board of the Royal Schools of Music

Three Friends Rag

Andy Hampton

© 2005 by The Associated Board of the Royal Schools of Music

AB 3140

Scherzo

Alan Haughton

© 2005 by The Associated Board of the Royal Schools of Music

AB 3140

Maigret

Martin Ellerby

© 2005 by The Associated Board of the Royal Schools of Music

The Village

Mark Lockheart

© 2005 by The Associated Board of the Royal Schools of Music

AB 3140

Country Gardens

Trad. English arr. Alan Haughton

© 2004 by The Associated Board of the Royal Schools of Music
This version © 2005 by The Associated Board of the Royal Schools of Music

AB 3140

A Dance Perchance?

Malcolm Miles

© 2005 by The Associated Board of the Royal Schools of Music

AB 3140

Carnival Shout

Alan Bullard

© 2005 by The Associated Board of the Royal Schools of Music

AB 3140

Closer Now

Jeffery Wilson

© 2005 by The Associated Board of the Royal Schools of Music

AB 3140

News Beat

Mark Goddard

© 2004 by The Associated Board of the Royal Schools of Music
This version © 2005 by The Associated Board of the Royal Schools of Music

AB 3140

Real Dreams

Andrew Wilson

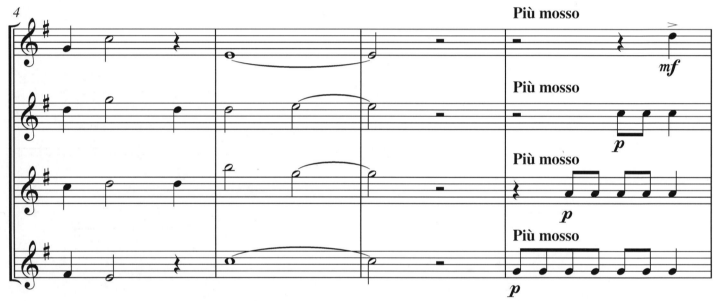

© 2005 by The Associated Board of the Royal Schools of Music

AB 3140